MERRY MOLE IS MAGIC

BY JUNE WOODMAN
ILLUSTRATED BY PAMELA STOREY

GONDOLA

Merry Mole is out for a walk in the forest. He sees the birds in the trees and the flowers under the trees. It is very cool in the forest. "I like it here," says Merry. He looks all round the cool, green forest. Then he sees something under a log. "What is under the log?" says Merry Mole.

Merry goes up to the log
to see what is there.
"It is a book!" he says.
He opens it and looks inside.
"Oh!" says Merry. "This
looks like a book of magic
spells. I will try one."
He reads it out loud.
"Magic spell, hear what I say.
Bring me some food right away."

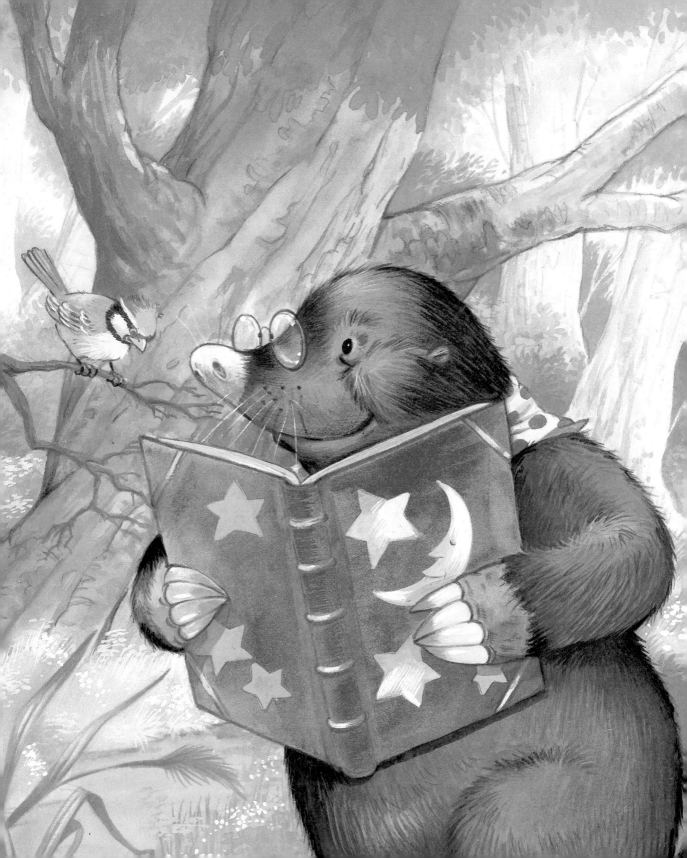

"Will it work?" says Merry.
He shuts his eyes and thinks
of all the food he likes best.
He thinks of ice-cream and
cakes. He thinks of apples
and oranges. He thinks of
puddings and pies.
"I am hungry," says Merry.
"I hope the magic spell
will work for me."

Merry opens his eyes and
sees Cuddly Cat. She is
out for a walk and she has
a big basket. Cuddly says,
"I have been baking cakes."
Merry can see that the basket
is full. Cuddly gives Merry
a cake.
"This is very good," says
Merry. "My magic spell works."
He tells Cuddly all about
the book.

"Oh! How clever," says Cuddly.
"You must be magic, Merry."
They walk out of the forest.
They sit on a seat by Bossy
Bear's house.
"Try the magic again," says
Cuddly Cat.
"It may not work," says Merry,
but he opens the book.
He reads it out loud.
"Magic spell, I really think
We would like a lovely drink."

Merry and Cuddly shut their
eyes. They begin to think of
all the drinks they like best.
"I like milk and cream,"
says Cuddly Cat.
"I like orange drinks," says
Merry, "and I like lemon ones
as well. Milk shakes are
very good too! I hope the
magic spell will work for
me this time."

Bossy Bear comes out of his house. He sees Merry Mole and Cuddly Cat.

"I have made some nice lemon drinks," says Bossy. "Come and try some." They go inside and try the lemon drinks.

"Thank you. What a lovely drink," says Cuddly. "You are magic, Merry."

They tell Bossy all about the book of spells.

They all set off down the lane.
"Try some more magic, Merry,"
says Bossy Bear.
"It may not work," says Merry,
but he opens the book.
He reads it out loud.
"Magic spell we want to play.
Please bring us a toy, today."
"What now?" says Bossy Bear.
"Sit and think of some good
toys," says Merry Mole.

So they sit down and shut
their eyes. They begin to
think. Bossy Bear thinks
of scooters and roller skates.
Cuddly Cat thinks of balloons
and dolls.
Merry Mole thinks of slides
and swings.
"I like all kinds of toys,"
says Bossy Bear.
"So do we," say Cuddly Cat
and Merry Mole.

Here comes Paddy Dog with
a big red ball.
"Come and play with me,"
says Paddy Dog.
"Merry is magic!" say Bossy
and Cuddly. They tell Paddy
about the book of spells.
"Try some more magic,"
says Paddy Dog.
"I am too tired," says Merry.
"Ask for a ride," says Paddy.
So Merry finds a good spell.

Here comes Hoppy Rabbit.
He is in his little car.
"Come for a ride," he says.
"Is that magic?" says Paddy.
They all get into the car and
tell Hoppy about the book.
When they get to the duck
pond, they tell Dilly Duck and
her three ducklings.
"Merry is magic!" say the
ducklings. "Try some magic
for us, please, Merry."

But Dilly Duck says, "You are all very silly. Merry Mole is NOT magic. That book is just for fun. I got it from the market for the ducklings to read, but I lost it in the forest."
Poor Merry. He is very sad.
"I liked being magic," he says.
"Do not be sad," says Cuddly.
"We had lots of fun."

Flippy Frog is by the pond.
"Come over here," he says.
They all run to look in the
duck pond.
"LOOK!" says Flippy. "The
tadpoles have lost their
tails. They are not tadpoles
now. They are baby frogs!"
"That is very clever," says
Dilly to the ducklings.
"Tadpoles are REAL magic!"
says Merry Mole.

Say these words again

walk

please

ask

shakes

would

tadpoles

hungry

think

oranges

slides

loud

swings

ice-cream

tired